STONE PIER
P R E S S

Stone Pier Press
San Francisco, California

ISBN: 978-0-9988623-0-9
Library of Congress Control Number: 2017960159
Names: Crawford, Leslie, author. Stangl, Sonja, illustrator. Ellis, Clare, editor.
Title: Sprig the Rescue Pig
Summary: Inspired by true events, Sprig is an uplifting tale about a little pig who changes his life by taking one giant leap – for ages 5 to 8.

Manufactured in China by Leo Paper Products, LTD.

10 9 8 7 6 5 4 3 2 1
First Printing: January 2018
Printed on Forest Stewardship Council (FSC) responsibly sourced paper from well-managed forests

FSC
www.fsc.org
MIX
Paper from
responsible sources
FSC® C020056

SPRIG

THE RESCUE PIG

Written by **Leslie Crawford**

Illustrated by **Sonja Stangl**

Sometimes you know things, even if you don't have words for them.

So even though he didn't have the words, our words, this is what Pig knew on that blazingly hot day as he sped along a country road in a truck jam-packed with lots of other unhappy pigs, most of them bigger than he was.

Pig knew that this was no life for a pig.

Without being braggy, Pig also knew he was pretty darn smart, and that's saying a lot. Why? Because pigs are very intelligent animals. He was also charming. All the other pigs told him so.

But what did smarts and charm matter if your life was miserable? Because Pig also knew he was very sad.

Just this morning he had left one unbearable pig-crammed space for another. Only this one was moving.

Until it stopped.

Screeeeeech!

The pigs bumped and rammed into one another and a chorus of grunts and shrieks erupted. **Eeeeeek! Oooffff! Eeeergh!**

Oh, the din! Then Pig tuned into an even bigger sound. A freight train passed in front of the truck. **Shoosh! Shoosh! Shoosh!!**

And then another noise. **"Arrrggggh!"** It was the truck driver who was annoyed about being late for his delivery.

But just as the commotion intensified, something quite strange and wonderful happened.

Amid the squeals and the screeches, the clamor and the chaos, the rest of the world suddenly fell away and became beautifully quiet.

For Pig, anyway.

Because he'd gotten wind of the most scrumptious scent ever.

Pig had caught a whiff of rich forest soil, ripe red
berries, crisp fresh leaves, and mouthwatering
mushrooms that hid among tree roots.

His finely attuned snout told him all that in just
a few sniffs, which was peculiar because he had
never in his life been outdoors.

Suddenly, Pig knew what he had to do.
He had to go after that smell.

Excuse me, pardon me, grunted Pig, as he slipped his limber young body through the crowd of pigs. He stopped for a moment and lifted his nose. *Sniff, sniff.*

It's out there.

He pushed and pressed and shoved his way to the edge of the truck, where he paused.

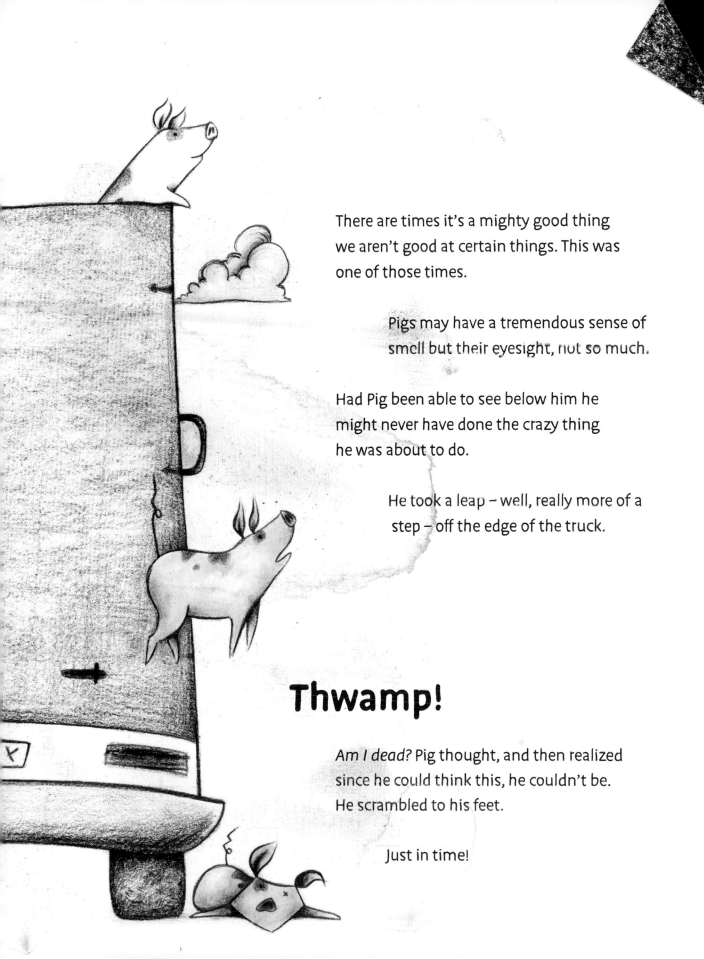

There are times it's a mighty good thing we aren't good at certain things. This was one of those times.

Pigs may have a tremendous sense of smell but their eyesight, not so much.

Had Pig been able to see below him he might never have done the crazy thing he was about to do.

He took a leap – well, really more of a step – off the edge of the truck.

Thwamp!

Am I dead? Pig thought, and then realized since he could think this, he couldn't be. He scrambled to his feet.

Just in time!

"What the...?!" It was the driver who was looking at Pig in his rearview mirror. He jumped out of his truck and charged at Pig.

Thump! Thump!

Yikes! Pig did what only a very scared pig could do. Run!

Run, Pig, run! the other pigs cheered. He almost stopped to look back at his friends, but the man was gaining on him. If he didn't get away now, it was bacon for him.

So Pig raced down a hill toward the rich forest-y smell and away from the driver's pounding footsteps.

Pig ran and ran and ran until he was absolutely certain he'd left the driver behind. Panting, he finally stopped and looked around. *Where am I?*

Sniff, Sniff. Ahhhhh!

Pig breathed in the deliciousness of the woods and felt the velvety, black soil under his hooves. He tossed a few oak leaves in the air and then discovered - *gasp!* - a tiny heap of tender, tasty acorns. Munching, he returned to the soft soil and rolled in it.

Is this hog heaven?
Indeed, it was.

But what's that? He'd caught
wind of something irresistible.
There! Right over that hill.

Pig took off in search of it.

Within moments, Pig found what he'd been smelling.
It sat on the middle of a blanket, just waiting for him
to eat it.

Pig went for it...at the very same time as a girl named Rory.

"Gaaah!" screamed Rory.

"Noooo!" yelled her mom.

Eeeek! yowled Pig.

That first meeting between Sprig and Rory could have ended right there. When a pig crashes your picnic it's pretty terrifying for everyone involved. But something altogether unexpected happened instead.

Rory held out her peanut butter and jelly sandwich. Pig swallowed it in one gulp.

Wow,
they both thought.

Pig's tail began wagging furiously. Rory leaned over and gently scratched the sensitive spot behind his ears.

More! thought Pig. He rolled over so Rory could reach his hard-to-get-to spots.

Rory's mom was taking in the whole scene.

She realized how unusual it was for a piglet
to be alone in the woods.

She understood how dangerous it could be.

She knew there was only one thing to do.

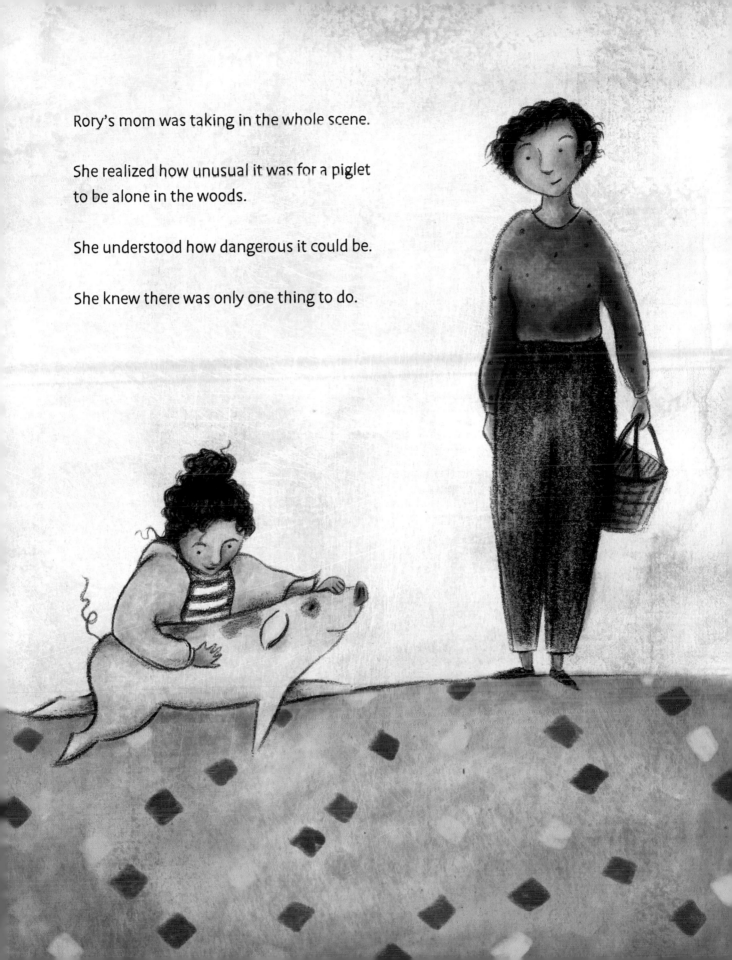

"It's time to go home," her mom said. Rory stopped scratching. Pig nuzzled her hand, hoping for more. "And the little guy comes with us."

"Yeeesss!!" Rory threw her arms around her mom.

Pig looked up at Rory. He knew something was happening. He wondered if it would taste good.

Rory picked up the picnic blanket and gently tied it around Pig's neck, like a leash.

"Come on, Pig!" she said. "Wait - we can't just call you Pig! How about Twig? Fig? Ummmm... Sprig? Yes, Sprig!"

Pig, well, Sprig, wagged his tail.

And just like that Sprig had a leash, a name and a person, who took him home in time for dinner.

The next day was Sunday for everyone else.
But for Rory it was Pig Day!

"Hello, Sprig!" Rory said. He looked at her expectantly.

"Okay! We'll go for a walk."

She tied the picnic blanket around the little pig's
neck and...

Whoa! thought Sprig, as they left the house.
So many smells! So many sounds!

Wait - what's that?

A scruffy white dog had stopped and was
sniffing him. Not knowing what else to do,
Sprig let him.

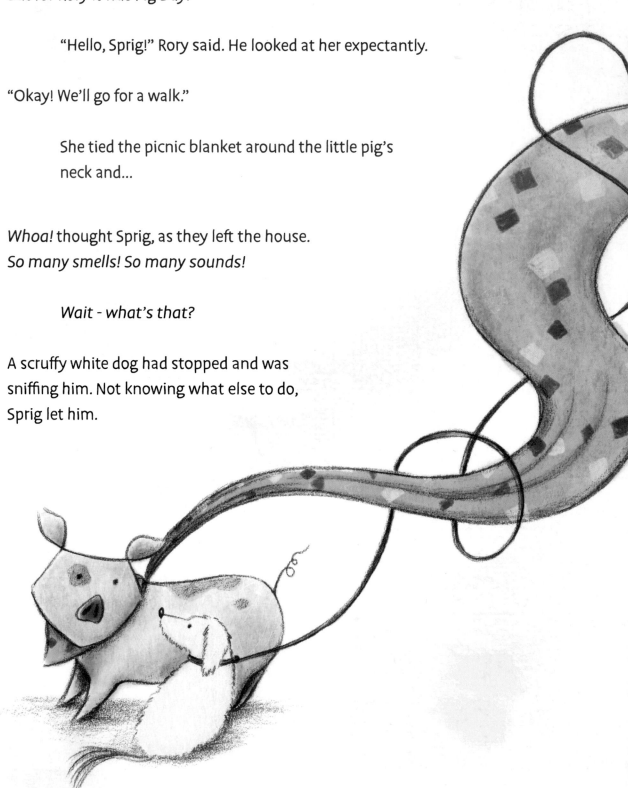

"I like your dog!" said Rory. "What's his name?"

"Bix," said the girl at the other end of the leash. "I found him running loose on the street. He's a rescue dog. I like your pig! What's his name?"

"Sprig," said Rory. "I found him running loose in the woods. I guess he's a rescue pig."

Sprig, who'd just caught a delectable new scent, wasn't listening. He tugged so hard on the picnic blanket leash that Rory had no choice but to follow him. "Hold on, Sprig!" she said. "See you later!" she called behind her.

The next day was Monday, which was definitely
not Pig Day.

"You need to go to school, Rory," said her mom.
"And I need to go to the office."

There was no point arguing.

Rory led Sprig to their backyard and gave him a
scratch. "Don't worry. I'll be back soon."

Sprig sat down, watching the spot where Rory had
disappeared. Then he poked his snout through the
fence.

But Rory was still gone.

He looked around the yard and found a ball. He
pushed it around, tossing it in the air. Then he rolled
in the grass a few times.

Looking towards the gate again he felt a little pang.

On Tuesday, after Rory left for school, Sprig tried cheering himself up by eating all the flowers in the yard.

On Wednesday, he dug holes all over the lawn looking for mushrooms or acorns. *Nothing! Harumph.*

On Friday, Sprig had an idea, a really good one if he did say so himself. He trotted to the gate and nuzzled it. In no time he'd lifted the latch and the gate swung open.

Whoo-hoo!

On Thursday, he rubbed up against a small tree so hard, trying to get at an itchy spot, that he brought it down. *Uh, oh.*

Sprig did a little pig jig out onto the street and...

Honk! Honk! Screeech!

A truck stopped inches from Sprig. The little pig froze.

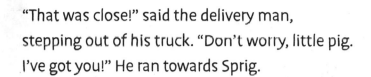

"That was close!" said the delivery man,
stepping out of his truck. "Don't worry, little pig.
I've got you!" He ran towards Sprig.

Thump! Thump!

That sound! For Sprig it meant only one thing,
and it wasn't good

He began running wildly in confused circles,
nearly blind with fear and the memory of what
he had escaped from.

But there. Sprig got a whiff of something, someone familiar, with just a hint of PB&J sandwich.

"Sprig!" Rory suddenly appeared before him.
"Sprig! Here I am."

He let out a high-pitched squeal of joy and pressed his trembling body against Rory.

"It's okay, Sprig. It's okay."

It is okay, Sprig thought.
Everything's all right now.

The two friends walked back to the house
where Rory's mom met them at the door.

"Hey," she said. "I have an idea."

On Saturday, Sprig woke up with a sense that something was different.

"Hi Sprig," Rory said quietly.

Worried, he followed her so closely he bumped into her as she moved around the kitchen, packing snacks in a bag.

Rory turned and gave him a nice, long scratch. "Come on, Sprig," she said. "We have to go."

She tied on his picnic blanket leash and led him to the car.

They drove for awhile. The aromas gradually shifted from city to country, from buses and buildings (yes, buildings have smells), to the sumptuous perfumes of the forests and the fields.

Sprig lay his head on Rory's lap and talked to himself in contented grunts, as pigs do when they're relaxed.

Then the car turned into a wide gate and stopped.

"We're here," said Rory's mom.

Sprig sat up in his seat and felt a tickle in his nose.

What a sweet scent! Was it...? Yes! Other pigs! And as pigs know
how to smell such things, he didn't smell fear. He smelled joy.

"Sprig will love it here," a man was saying. "Plenty of pig friends.
Mud baths. And Tuesday is mashed potato night." He reached down
to Sprig and gave him a rub behind his ears. *Oh,* thought Sprig,
smiling. *Nice!*

Rory held the end of the picnic blanket leash close for a moment,
and then passed it to the man...

... who took it from her gently.

He walked Sprig to a nearby pasture filled with grass and *oh so many
pigs!* These pigs weren't crowded in small pens. They were outside in
the sunshine, moving where they liked and chatting, as pigs do.

Sprig looked back at Rory. *I don't want to leave her. But look at those pigs!*

He took a few small steps. Then – he couldn't help himself – he broke into a run. *Hello pigs!*

"Sprig!" Rory called. He stopped and turned around. "I'll see you soon. I promise!"

Rory was quiet as they drove away. Then her mom said, "We have one more stop to make before we get home."

They took the exit just before their usual one and pulled up in front of a tan building.

Inside, her mom approached a woman standing at a counter. "My daughter is ready for a pet," she said. "Anyone here in need of a friend?"

"I know just the dog," said the woman. "Come meet Sprog."

More about pigs

Like Sprig, a domestic pig starts out small and cute. But fully grown they can get to be between 600 and 1000 pounds! It's one big reason farm pigs don't make good indoor pets.

Pigs are considered highly intelligent and, by some measures, as smart as dogs, dolphins, and chimpanzees. Pigs can even be taught to play video games using a joystick.

Just like a dog, pigs can be taught to recognize their names and come when called. They can also be trained to walk on a leash, use a litter box, and perform many tricks. They love having their bellies rubbed, too.

Thanks to their highly curious natures, *sus domesticus* (the formal name for a pig) are bored easily and get stressed out if stuck in small spaces with not enough to do.

Pigs love to play! Just for the fun of it, they will chase one another, push balls, ring bells, throw hay in the air, and jump and hop.

Pigs are very social animals and prefer to be with other pigs. A group of young pigs is called a drift, drove, or litter and a group of older pigs is called a sounder of swine. When they sleep, they doze in a pig pile, tucked in close to each other.

Pigs frequently talk to each other with more than 30 different oinks, grunts, and squeals. They can be as loud as a chainsaw. Some farmers wear earmuffs to protect their ears from the squeals! A piglet can recognize his mother's voice at two weeks old and mama pigs sing to their babies.

A pig has an excellent sense of olfaction (smell!), with a finely-tuned nose that helps them find food, including truffles as deep as three feet underground.

Despite their reputation, pigs are very clean and prefer not to soil (as in, pee or poo in) their living areas. They bathe in water and love to swim. Also, they don't *sweat like pigs*. Because they can't sweat, they like to wallow in mud to cool off.

An adult pig can run up to 11 miles per hour...fast!

Pigs are very sensitive and can empathize. They easily pick up on what another pig is feeling, for instance. As with dogs and cats – and humans! – they have unique personalities and cycle in and out of good and bad moods.

Sprig's story is loosely based on a real pig who leaped off a delivery truck and was lucky enough to end up in an animal sanctuary.

Thanks to the following good people for reviewing *More about pigs*:
Katherine Keefe, shelter director, Woodstock Farm Sanctuary
Sy Montgomery, author, *The Good Good Pig*
Lauri Torgerson-White, senior animal welfare specialist, Mercy For Animals
Leslie Smith, animal welfare journalist